SPORTS BIOGRAPHIES

KOBE BRYANT

LAKERS

24

KENNY ABDO

Fly!
An Imprint of Abdo Zoom
abdobooks.com

abdobooks.com

Published by Abdo Zoom, a division of ABDO, P.O. Box 398166, Minneapolis,
Minnesota 55439. Copyright © 2021 by Abdo Consulting Group, Inc. International
copyrights reserved in all countries. No part of this book may be reproduced in any
form without written permission from the publisher. Fly!™ is a trademark and logo
of Abdo Zoom.

Printed in China.
052020
092020

**THIS BOOK CONTAINS
RECYCLED MATERIALS**

Photo Credits: AP Images, Getty Images, Icon Sportswire, iStock, Shutterstock
Production Contributors: Kenny Abdo, Jennie Forsberg, Grace Hansen
Design Contributors: Dorothy Toth, Neil Klinepier

Library of Congress Control Number: 2019956180

Publisher's Cataloging-in-Publication Data

Names: Abdo, Kenny, author.
Title: Kobe Bryant / by Kenny Abdo
Description: Minneapolis, Minnesota : Abdo Zoom, 2021 | Series: Sports biographies |
    Includes online resources and index.
Identifiers: ISBN 9781098221386 (lib. bdg.) | ISBN 9781098222369 (ebook) |
    ISBN 9781098222857 (Read-to-Me ebook)
Subjects: LCSH: Bryant, Kobe, 1978-2020 ---Juvenile literature. | Professional athletes
    -United States--Biography--Juvenile literature. | Basketball players--United
    States--Biography--Juvenile literature. | African American basketball players-
    Biography--Juvenile literature.
Classification: DDC 796.323092 [B]--dc23

TABLE OF CONTENTS

KOBE BRYANT

Kobe Bryant was a legendary small forward on the LA Lakers for 20 **seasons**.

An NBA **MVP** with many **championship** wins, two **Olympic** gold medals, and an unstoppable drive, Kobe Bryant is one of the greatest players in basketball history.

EARLY YEARS

Kobe Bryant was born in
Philadelphia, Pennsylvania, in 1978.

Bryant grew up in Italy where his father, Joe Bryant, played basketball. Kobe's passion for the sport grew during his time there.

After returning to Philadelphia, Bryant played basketball in high school. He led the team to the state **championships** four years in a row.

1996 PIAA CLASS AAAA STATE CHAMPIONS!

Kobe Bryant leads Aces to first state title since 1943

GOING PRO

Bryant was **drafted** into the NBA right after high school. He was the 13th overall pick for the Charlotte Hornets in 1996. The LA Lakers traded for him that same year. He was just 17 at the time.

At 19, Bryant became the youngest player to start in an NBA **All-Star Game** in the history of the sport.

Bryant and the US Team won the Gold medal over Spain at the 2008 **Olympics**. USA won its second gold medal with Bryant against Spain in 2012.

In his 20 **seasons** with the Lakers, Bryant lead the team to seven NBA **championships**. The team took home the O'Brien Trophy five times!

Bryant **retired** at the end of the 2015 **season**. In his last game, he scored an amazing 60 points, beating the Utah Jazz.

LEGACY

In 2007, Bryant and his wife started the Kobe & Vanessa Bryant Foundation. It gifts life changing experiences to less fortunate children.

Bryant, his daughter Gigi, and seven others passed away in a tragic helicopter crash on January 26, 2020. They were on their way to the Mamba Sports Academy for a game. Even in death, Bryant empowers and educates youth through the Academy, proving he wasn't just a legend on the court.

GLOSSARY

All-Star Game – yearly game played in February by the best 24 players from the National Basketball Association (NBA).

championship – a game held to find a first-place winner.

draft – a process in sports to assign athletes to a certain team.

MVP – in sports, a most valuable player (MVP) award is given to the best-performing athlete.

Olympic games – the biggest sporting event in the world that is divided into summer and winter games.

retire – leave one's career.

season – the portion of the year where certain games are played.

ONLINE RESOURCES

Booklinks
NONFICTION NETWORK
FREE! ONLINE NONFICTION RESOURCES

To learn more about
Kobe Bryant, please visit
abdobooklinks.com or scan
this QR code. These links
are routinely monitored
and updated to provide the
most current information
available.

INDEX